Walt Disney's
The Sword in the Stone

Senior Designer: Elaine Lopez
Editor: Sharon Fass Yates
Editorial Director: Pamela Pia

Walt Disney's The Sword in the Stone copyright © 1963, 2006 Disney Enterprises, Inc.
Story adapted by Carl Memling suggested by the original story,
"The Sword in the Stone," by T. H. White. Illustrations adapted by Norm McGary.

Copyright ©2008 Disney Enterprises, Inc. All Rights Reserved.
Published by Reader's Digest Children's Books,
Reader's Digest Road, Pleasantville, NY U.S.A. 10570-7000
and Reader's Digest Children's Publishing Limited,
The Ice House, 124-126 Walcot Street, Bath UK BA1 5BG
Reader's Digest Children's Books, the Pegasus logo,
and Reader's Digest are all registered trademarks of
The Reader's Digest Association, Inc. Manufactured in China.
1 3 5 7 9 10 8 6 4 2

Walt Disney's

The Sword in the Stone

Illustrated by The Walt Disney Studios
Adapted by Norm McGary

Story adapted by Carl Memling
suggested by the original story,
"The Sword in the Stone," by T. H. White

Reader's Digest Children's Books™

Pleasantville, New York • Montréal, Québec • Bath, United Kingdom

Wart was a lowly page living in the great stone castle of Sir Ector. Nobody called Wart by his proper name, which was Arthur. Everybody called him just "Wart."

Sir Ector had a big, lazy son named Kay, who liked
to stretch out in the sun and doze. His favorite spot
was a grassy bank near the drawbridge.

But poor Wart had to work and work.
He scrubbed pans and scoured pots in the castle
cookhouse.

He helped the castle carpenter.

He polished armor for the armorer.

He swept the castle stables clean.

Poor Wart. He was all tired out.

But one day there was a clap of thunder in the great hall of the castle.

There was a puff of smoke—and there stood a strange old man.

"My name is Merlin. I am a wizard," he said. "Wart needs lessons. So I have come."

Sir Ector and Kay laughed and hooted.

"Lessons! What does Wart need lessons for? Go away, old man," said Sir Ector.

Merlin waved his wand.
And right there inside the great hall it began to snow!
It snowed and it snowed and it snowed.
Well, Sir Ector soon changed his mind.
He let Merlin stay on, and said,
"Give Wart lessons, if you like."

Nobody understood why Wart needed lessons, but Merlin began to give him lessons.

He led him down to the moat one day.

And Merlin waved his wand.

Wart began to shrink. He shrank smaller and smaller.
Suddenly he changed into a little fish, and fell into
the water.

At first it was great fun.

But then a big fish came along.
The big fish wanted to catch the little fish for lunch.
Poor little Wart. What could he do?

He used his head.

He hid in a clump of weeds so the big fish couldn't find him.

"Very good," said Merlin. "You learned your lesson, Wart. *When in trouble, use your head.*"

Merlin kept on with the lessons.
Once he changed Wart into a squirrel.
As a squirrel, Wart stored nuts in trees.
He learned to be ready for what tomorrow might bring.

Another time Merlin changed him into a bird.

As a bird, Wart flew high in the sky.

And seeing the world from way up there, he learned many things.

Wart grew wiser and wiser.

But still nobody understood. Why did Wart need lessons?

One wintry day a knight came to the castle. He brought news of a great tournament to be held in London. The winner would be crowned king of all England.

"A tournament's the very thing we need to choose an English king," said Sir Ector.

He thought that Kay would win.

And so they all rode off.

Kay sat on a prancing horse. His armor glistened in the sunlight.

But Wart was just a lowly squire. He rode a plodding donkey all the way to London town.

After many days and many nights they came at last
to the tournament field.

There was a blast of trumpets.

And the tilting started.

Kay smiled proudly. Soon, with spear and sword, he
would fight to win the crown.

Suddenly, Wart ran from the field. He had forgotten
Kay's sword.

It was back at the inn where they had slept.

Wart ran as fast as he could. But when he got to the
inn, it was closed.

Poor Wart—where could he find a sword?
He ran and he ran.
In a churchyard he saw a marble stone.
On it stood a steel anvil.
And stuck through the anvil was a gleaming sword.

A sword!

Wart quickly pulled it out, and quickly carried it back
to the tournament field.

"But that's not Kay's sword!" cried Sir Ector when he
saw it.

Then he saw some letters written in gold on the sword.

This is what the letters said:

WHOSO PULLETH OUT THIS SWORD OF THIS STONE AND ANVIL IS RIGHTWISE KING BORN OF ALL ENGLAND.

Sir Ector read that. And so did all the other noblemen.

Now they knew. The tournament *wasn't* the thing whereby to choose a king. *This sword was!*

But how could Wart have pulled it out? There must be some mistake.

They all went to the churchyard.
Wart put back the sword into the stone.
Everyone tried, but the sword wouldn't move.
Only Wart could pull it out again. So it was no mistake.
But kings must be wise. Kings must know many things.
How could Wart be a king?

Wart was wise enough. And he knew enough.

For that's what the lessons had been for—to prepare Wart to be king.

And Wart became a great king, known forever after as King Arthur.